Jellybean Books

Three Little Kittens

Illustrated by Lilian Obligado

Random House 🏠 New York

Copyright © 1974 by Random House, Inc. All rights reserved.
Originally published in different form in 1974 as a Random House PICTUREBACK® Book.
First Random House Jellybean Books™ edition, 1998.
Library of Congress Catalog Card Number: 98-65518
ISBN: 0-679-89210-9 (trade); 0-679-99210-3 (lib. bdg.)
www.randomhouse.com/kids/
Printed in the United States of America 10 9 8 7 6 5 4 3 2 1
JELLYBEAN BOOKS is a trademark of Random House, Inc.

Three little kittens,
They lost their mittens,

And they began
to cry,

"Oh, mother dear, we sadly fear
Our mittens we have lost."

"What! Lost your mittens,
       You naughty kittens!

Then you shall have no pie."

"Mee-ow, mee-ow, mee-ow."

"No, you shall have no pie."

The three little kittens,
They found their mittens,

And they began
        to cry,

"Oh, mother dear, see here, see here,
        Our mittens we have found."

"What! Found your mittens,
Then you're good kittens!
Now you can have some pie."

"Purr-r, purr-r, purr-r,

Yes, yes, let's have some pie."

The three little kittens
Put on their mittens,

And soon ate up the pie.

"Oh, mother dear, we greatly fear
Our mittens we have soiled."

"What! Soiled your mittens,
You naughty kittens!"
Then they began to sigh,
"Mee-ow, mee-ow, mee-ow."
Then they began to sigh.

The three little kittens,
They washed their mittens,
And hung them out to dry.

"Oh, mother dear, do you not hear,
Our mittens we have washed!"

"What! Washed your mittens,
Then you're good kittens!
But I smell a rat close by."
"Mee-ow, mee-ow, mee-ow."
"Yes, I smell a rat close by."